Wuthering Heights

Written by Emily Brontë

Retold by Emma Carroll

Illustrated by Arpad Olbey

Collins

Part One
Chapter 1

By the time you read this account of my life, I'll be dead.
For the past 30 years I've lived at Wuthering Heights.
My sole purpose on earth has been revenge. Now, as I lie
dying, I know there's no joy in hate. And you, who called
me Heathcliff, need know this isn't all I am.

  I was born in a place that wasn't England. It was a land
of mountains and eagles and deep winter snows. I had
a mother who carried me on her back, and a father who
sang by our campfire.

When I was seven, the Englishmen came. They brought gifts of pocket watches and necklaces. Father said not to be fooled by their generosity: what they wanted was our land, and land made people greedy.

"Don't bow to those men," Father said. "Don't make yourself smaller than they are."

The land belonged to us and to Nature, he said.
No amount of money or threats would make us give it up.

Yet the English also brought us a disease: measles. It spread through my people like fire, my own parents dying of it within days. In our camp, I was one of few who survived. The Englishmen took our land anyway, and ordered me to work on it as a slave. But I remembered Father's words and knew I must stand tall.

So I fled to the sea. Hiding amongst bales of cotton, I boarded a ship bound for England. From that moment, I vowed never to bow to anyone. I'd claim back all that England had taken from me. I'd not stop until it was done.

The journey took 26 long days. I drank only rainwater and dined on rat flesh. And I read over and over two words written on the cloth that wrapped the cotton bales.

Linton. Earnshaw.

They were cotton traders' names. I didn't know then how important they would become.

By the time we reached England, I was half-mad with hunger. Liverpool Docks was a noisy, stinking place, full of men shouting and ropes heaving cargo high into the air. I had no shoes, no money. My empty belly ached. Though I reminded myself of what England owed me, I still felt cold and alone.

On the quayside, I noticed a man in a smart coat checking over the cotton. Our ship's captain went to him and shook his hand.

"Your share's all there, Mr Earnshaw," he said.

Earnshaw.

That name again.

This Mr Earnshaw reminded me bitterly of every Englishman I'd ever met. He was a cotton trader, and because of him people wanted land in countries like mine. Really I should hate him on the spot.

Yet when I saw a street boy edge towards him and slip a hand into his pocket, it was me who cried, "Stop! Thief!"

The boy escaped having stolen only a horsewhip and some apples. Mr Earnshaw was shaken but unharmed. He told me the whip had been a present for his daughter, Cathy, the fruit for his housemaid, Nelly.

"Thank you," he said, for his wallet was untouched. So too was the violin he'd brought for Hindley, his son. "How can I repay you?"

Yet I cursed myself for raising the alarm. I should have kept quiet and let him be robbed, just as my family had been.

So when Mr Earnshaw offered to buy me supper, I knew it wasn't enough. I was here to seek revenge on the English. It made sense to start with him.

So I told him I'd no home or family. It wasn't hard to cry a few tears.

"Take me home with you," I pleaded. "Don't leave me all alone."

He wasn't sure at first, but I was able to convince him, and eventually he said, "Very well. Come with me."

All day we travelled by stagecoach. By sundown
the road became too narrow for the carriage. So we
walked the last ten miles, climbing onto the moor along
a steep path marked with white stones.

His home, Mr Earnshaw said, was called Wuthering
Heights. It loomed from the hillside, its windows lit
by candlelight.

"Marvellous! They've waited up for my return!"
Mr Earnshaw exclaimed.

And he led me inside.

Chapter 2

The first things I saw were a great flaming fire and a dresser stacked with plates. Two children – Cathy and Hindley, I supposed – threw themselves at Mr Earnshaw, who collapsed laughing into a chair.

Cathy soon discovered her present of a horsewhip was lost. She stamped her foot and clenched her fists with anger. I liked her spirit. It was fiercer than that of her brother who, when he saw how our rough journey had wrecked his violin, burst into silly tears.

Then all eyes fell on me. Cathy grinned, but Mrs Earnshaw flew into a rage.

"How could you bring him here? We've already enough mouths to feed!" she cried.

When Mr Earnshaw explained how he owed me, his wife grew calmer. She ordered Nelly the maid to wash me and find some clean clothes. But Mrs Earnshaw never took to me, nor I to her. When she died a few months later, it was no loss to me.

That night I slept out on the landing since neither Cathy nor Hindley wanted to share their rooms. All the next day, they called me "it", though only when their father was out of earshot. It puzzled me at first, but I soon learnt it was the Englishman's way to look down on outsiders.

Yet before long, Cathy and I became friends. She had a wildness in her that matched the wildness in me. She said my name should be Heathcliff – it'd belonged to a brother who died some years before. Mr Earnshaw was delighted. He saw that dead child in me, he said, and that brought him happiness.

So Heathcliff I became. It served as my first and surname, and as the months passed, then the years, Wuthering Heights became my home. Often I'd gaze out over the countryside and think of the life I'd left behind. Here, the moors belonged to the Earnshaws, and the land beyond to that other name I knew: Linton. Both made money from cotton. One day, I decided, all this land would be mine.

With Mr Earnshaw's strong attachment to me, I hoped he'd leave Wuthering Heights to me in his will. Then I'd get revenge the easy way, without having to lift a finger.

Meanwhile, my presence ate away at Hindley, who knew I was his father's favourite and despised me more each day. When no one was looking, he'd punch and kick me, but I wouldn't give him the satisfaction of fighting back – not yet.

Eventually, Hindley was sent away to college. Then, one stormy night, Mr Earnshaw died peacefully in his chair by the fire. Cathy and I cried many tears. Yet on discovering he'd left Wuthering Heights to Hindley, not me, my tears stopped. Revenge hadn't come easily, after all. But it would come, of that I was certain.

Chapter 3

Hindley came home for his father's funeral, bringing with him a new wife. Our old differences weren't forgotten. Banishing me to the servants' quarters, he said I must be treated like any other lad on the farm. It was the bitterest blow. Without Mr Earnshaw's protection, I was quickly reduced to nothing.

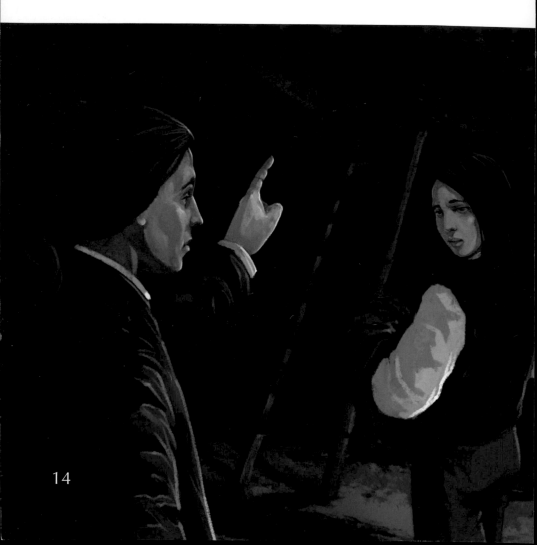

My one consolation was Cathy. We'd grown into young people who knew their own minds; we both hated Hindley with a passion. When we weren't plotting his downfall, we'd escape to the moors and run amongst the harebells or climb Penistone Craggs. It was my only happiness.

One Sunday evening, Cathy and I tricked Hindley by pouring pond water into his soup. For punishment we were locked inside the washhouse. Needless to say we escaped through the window, and headed straight for the moors. It was a windy, moonlit night. From the highest point we looked down into the valley and saw the many lights of Thrushcross Grange.

"I wonder how they spend their Sunday evenings?" sighed Cathy. She meant the Lintons who lived there, and who, I was certain, had never run across the moors even in daylight.

"Let's find out," I said.

We charged down the hillside, stopping only when we reached Thrushcross Grange. The gates were bolted, yet we crawled through the hedge and followed a path towards the house, where lights blazed from every window. To our delight the shutters remained open, so we were able to peer inside.

"Oh, Heathcliff!" Cathy gasped. "It looks like heaven!"

There were red carpets, gold tables, lamps hanging like jewels from the ceiling. Amongst these riches, a boy and girl stood weeping.

Cathy frowned. "That's Isabella and Edgar Linton. I can't think why they'd be crying."

"Because they're silly, spoilt things," I remarked.

Cathy and I laughed and made ghostly noises at the window, which frightened the snivelling pair into more tears.

Suddenly, a man with a dog appeared. We took fright and ran, but the dog was faster and brought Cathy to the ground. By the time the man reached us, I'd wrestled the dog off but Cathy's ankle bled alarmingly. She looked sick with pain.

On discovering us, the man
lifted Cathy over his shoulder
and took her inside. I stayed
close by. But at the door,
Mr Linton himself blocked my
entrance. He looked so much
the English gentleman,
I felt anger rise up in my throat.

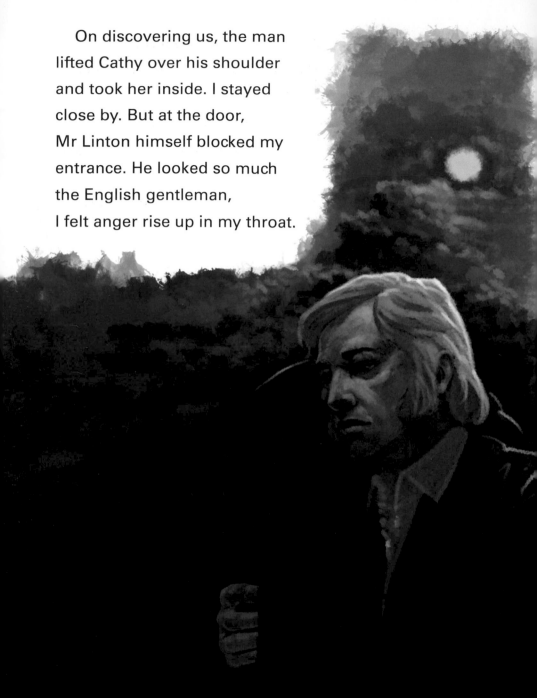

"Why, the boy looks like a villain," he observed.

His wife put on her spectacles to peer at me, and their cowardly children crept nearer.

"Frightful thing!" squealed the girl, Isabella.

"He must be the strange creature Mr Earnshaw brought home from Liverpool," said Mr Linton.

I hated how he gazed at me as if I was an exotic insect. I hated his wide-eyed family too. But I wouldn't leave without Cathy.

In the end, they had to throw me out, but not before I'd glimpsed Cathy through the window. She lay on a sofa, surrounded by Lintons. They'd bandaged her foot and given her cakes to eat, and when she laughed they smiled in delight.

Back at the Heights, I expected a thrashing. But Hindley had devised a harsher punishment: on Cathy's return I was forbidden to speak to her. One word and I'd be sent away. So I kept my head down, did my work, and my taste for revenge grew stronger than ever.

Chapter 4

Five weeks later, Cathy came home. When she appeared riding side-saddle, I felt I was looking at a stranger. The Cathy I knew rode horses like a boy: this girl wore spotless clothes and her hair fell in curls like Isabella Linton's. Yet Hindley was delighted with his sister's new appearance. Lifting her from her horse, he announced she was "quite a beauty".

Silent and sad,
I went back to my work.
Next to Cathy I looked
like a beggar boy from
the Liverpool docks,
and felt very ashamed.
Later, when she found
me she grabbed my
hands. But her smile
quickly became a frown,
for my fingers were
filthy and had made her
fancy gloves dirty.

"You don't need to touch me," I snapped, pulling
my hands away.

In private, I shed bitter tears. One by one those I loved
had deserted me – my parents, Mr Earnshaw, now Cathy.
I'd never felt so alone.

So the next day, I came up with a new plan.

"Nelly, make me decent," I said to the housemaid.

While she brushed my clothes, I scrubbed myself until
the water turned grey. I'd never be Edgar Linton but I
could smarten myself up. And with land, I'd become rich –
this I had to remember.

"'You look fit for a prince," said Nelly, when I was done.
Yet Hindley, on seeing me, shoved me back into
the kitchen. That wretched Edgar Linton was with him,
and he smirked at my newly combed hair. I couldn't bear
it. Grabbing a bowl of hot apple sauce, I threw it over him.
Needless to say, I got a thrashing. Later, as I sat staring
miserably into the fire, I promised myself that Hindley
Earnshaw would one day feel my hatred. Thinking of it
made me feel better.

Summer brought a son for Hindley and his wife. They called him Hareton, after the first Earnshaw to live at Wuthering Heights and whose name, with the date 1500, was carved above the front door. Yet Hindley's wife soon died, her loss making him sink into black despair. I knew of such loss, but unlike Hindley who let it swallow him, I'd used mine to give me purpose.

In his misery, Hindley forgot to keep Cathy and me apart; he had little need. For Cathy, a fine young woman now who wore silk frocks, spent more time with the Lintons than with me. One day, I mentioned how quickly she'd forgotten our friendship.

She laughed wickedly. "Why would I spend time with you, Heathcliff? Compared to Isabella and Edgar you're no company at all!"

I stormed out of the kitchen just as Edgar Linton came in, looking sleek and smart. The sight of him filled me with spite. But I was beginning to realise that while I was a rough, wild creature, he was a gentleman from his coat to his boots.

And that gave him power.

A few days later, Hindley was – as usual – in a terrible temper. So Nelly, Hareton and I gathered by the fire and waited for it to pass. Cathy joined us, not realising I was present, as I sat apart from the others. She spoke about Edgar, about his land and wealth and how if she married him, she'd be the finest lady in the district. Her talk angered me.

How could she care for such a weakling? How could she think Thrushcross Grange better than Wuthering Heights?

"My future is with Edgar," she said. "It would embarrass me to be seen with Heathcliff now."

Her words were poison to my ears.

Once my family had been great people too. Then the Englishmen came with their greed and disease, men who wanted cotton like the Lintons and the Earnshaws. To them I was nothing: Cathy thought the same.

In that moment, I knew how to seek revenge. I'd look and dress as an Englishman. I'd learn his cheating ways. And where better to do so than amongst those cotton traders who'd started this whole shameful business.

As Cathy kept talking, I tiptoed out of the kitchen and disappeared into the night.

Part Two
Chapter 5

After three years of hard work and cunning,
my transformation was complete. I was no longer a farm
boy or a beggar. I returned to Wuthering Heights a
fully-grown man, looking every inch the gentleman.
My desire for revenge burnt stronger than ever,
but from now on I'd do things the Englishman's way.
Money was my only weapon.

At Wuthering Heights, I learnt Cathy had married that pathetic creature Edgar Linton. The news sickened me. So too did the state of the house, once proud and homely, and now as dirty as a cave. Its occupants, Hindley and his son, Hareton, were equally filthy.

"So you have money now," my old enemy Hindley said, greedily eyeing my good coat and leather boots. He told me he'd lost all his wealth through poor business deals; I took great delight in hearing it.

Later, I went to Thrushcross Grange so Cathy could see the rich man I'd become. My arrival shocked Nelly, who now worked as housemaid at the Grange. I begged her to fetch Cathy at once.

When Cathy appeared so excited to see me, I softened. She'd not forgotten me after all. And so, I decided, my war wouldn't be with her. When she invited me inside, her husband was less welcoming. It amused me to observe how weak looking he was. To think I'd once envied his light hair! In return, he stared at me coolly. He'd rather I took my tea with the servants, I knew, but those days were gone.

I visited the Grange often. There was joy in seeing Cathy again. Yet I took greater delight in how my presence angered Edgar. Revenge against penniless Hindley seemed too easy. Edgar, with his huge house and parkland, was more of a prize.

Within a month or so, the opportunity to settle old scores presented itself. I'd become a fine-looking man, as my father had also been. Isabella Linton seemed to agree and took to giggling in my presence. Cathy mocked her for it. I, though, could hardly hide my delight, for Isabella would inherit her brother's entire fortune when he died. Cathy didn't approve of my growing interest in Isabella. One afternoon, we had a vicious argument. Edgar became involved. Though the weakling looked faint with fear, he banned me from visiting his house ever again. It only served to make me more determined.

The next night, I told Isabella to meet me in the woods nearby. She came, the fool, and we rode away as fast as the rough roads would allow. Early the next morning, we married.

On returning to Wuthering Heights, my new wife, Mrs Heathcliff, realised her mistake. The house was a dirty, miserable place compared to the Grange, and she realised how little I loved her.

"This marriage was a trick!" Isabella sobbed. "You married me just to anger Edgar."

Indeed, she was right.

Hindley also realised I'd not share my wealth with him, and went back to despising me. He took his temper out on his son. Poor Hareton didn't know what he'd done to deserve this, and I used his hurt to my advantage. I sided with the boy, and enjoyed teaching him to disrespect his father. Soon we were friends.

Meanwhile, in marrying his sister, I had indeed angered Edgar Linton. He refused any contact with us and forbade Cathy from visiting. Isabella wrote him long, pleading letters, but I believe the only one to read them was Nelly, and one day, by way of reply, she came to Wuthering Heights. Her purpose was to check on Isabella's welfare. But I wanted news of Cathy.

"Ever since you argued that day, she's been dangerously ill," Nelly said. "So if you really care, you'll leave her alone."

She couldn't expect this. Not of me.

"I mean it, Heathcliff. The master forbids it. Her health is very fragile. Another meeting with you will be too much for her," Nelly said.

"Nonsense! I must see her," I replied, and insisted Nelly find a way to smuggle me into Thrushcross Grange.

The chance came on a Sunday when Edgar was at church. At the Grange, I found Cathy sitting quietly with a book. It'd been months since I'd seen her; she'd grown thin and frail. It shocked me greatly. Yet it was clear she was going to have a baby, and I felt sure, in her weakened state, she'd not survive the birth.

On seeing me, she smiled sadly. "My truest friend," she said. "How I wish we'd never been parted."

Between us, we cried many tears. Our friendship had been tested these last months. Yet once again it had survived. Having lost so much in my life, I couldn't imagine now losing Cathy as well.

Early the next morning, Nelly told me Cathy had given birth to a daughter, whose name was Catherine. As I'd feared, my poor Cathy hadn't survived. Nelly sobbed, yet I was past tears. This was an agony I couldn't bear. Edgar Linton was to blame. He'd taken Cathy's spirit and snuffed it out like a candle. I despised him now more than ever.

Before the funeral, I visited Cathy as she lay in her coffin. She had a locket around her neck; inside it was a piece of Edgar's hair. Throwing his blonde strands to the floor, I replaced them with a dark curl of my own.

My revenge was just beginning.

Chapter 6

With Cathy dead, my heart turned to stone. One night in a rage, I told Isabella to leave. My wife took off in a snowstorm with our unborn child. Months later, I heard from Nelly that she'd settled in the city and had our son, named Linton.

"She wants me to hate him," I said, for why else would she give him her family's name?

Then, not six months after Cathy's death, Hindley Earnshaw died with debts so vast only I could clear them. Wuthering Heights had finally become mine. Hindley's son, Hareton, was left nothing, yet he stayed fiercely loyal to me, his father's enemy.

Money – my weapon of revenge – was working. It was now time to set my sights on Thrushcross Grange.

I waited 12 years for my next chance to torment Edgar Linton. It came with the news that Isabella had died. Linton Heathcliff, my son, had gone to stay with his uncle at the Grange. He'd be happier there, but I didn't want him happy. So I summoned him to live with me at Wuthering Heights.

Nelly brought Linton early one morning. Though he was a boy of 12, he clung to her like a baby. "What a charming thing!" I sneered, wondering how such a sickly lad could be any son of mine.

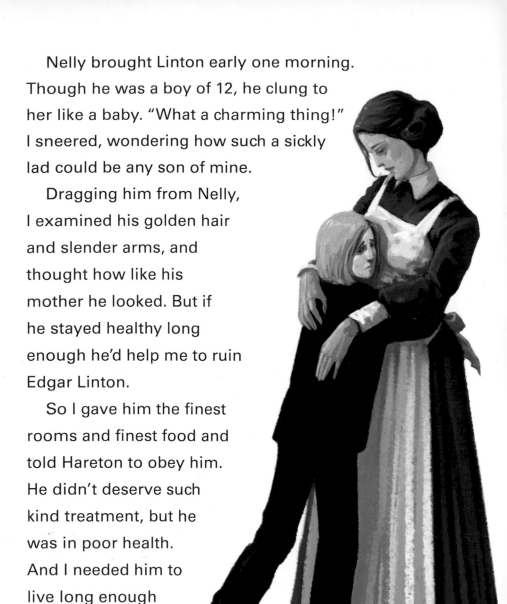

Dragging him from Nelly, I examined his golden hair and slender arms, and thought how like his mother he looked. But if he stayed healthy long enough he'd help me to ruin Edgar Linton.

So I gave him the finest rooms and finest food and told Hareton to obey him. He didn't deserve such kind treatment, but he was in poor health. And I needed him to live long enough to marry.

Despite many illnesses, Linton grew to be a young man.
Not four miles away at the Grange his cousin Catherine,
the baby born to Cathy, was now a young woman.
I'd often watch her from a distance on the moors. She bore
no resemblance to her mother, but like my son, she had
Edgar's blonde hair and for that I despised her, too.

One day, Catherine and Nelly wandered onto my land.
I asked Catherine if she'd like to meet her cousin.

Nelly resisted. "Her father would hate it!"

Which of course was my plan.

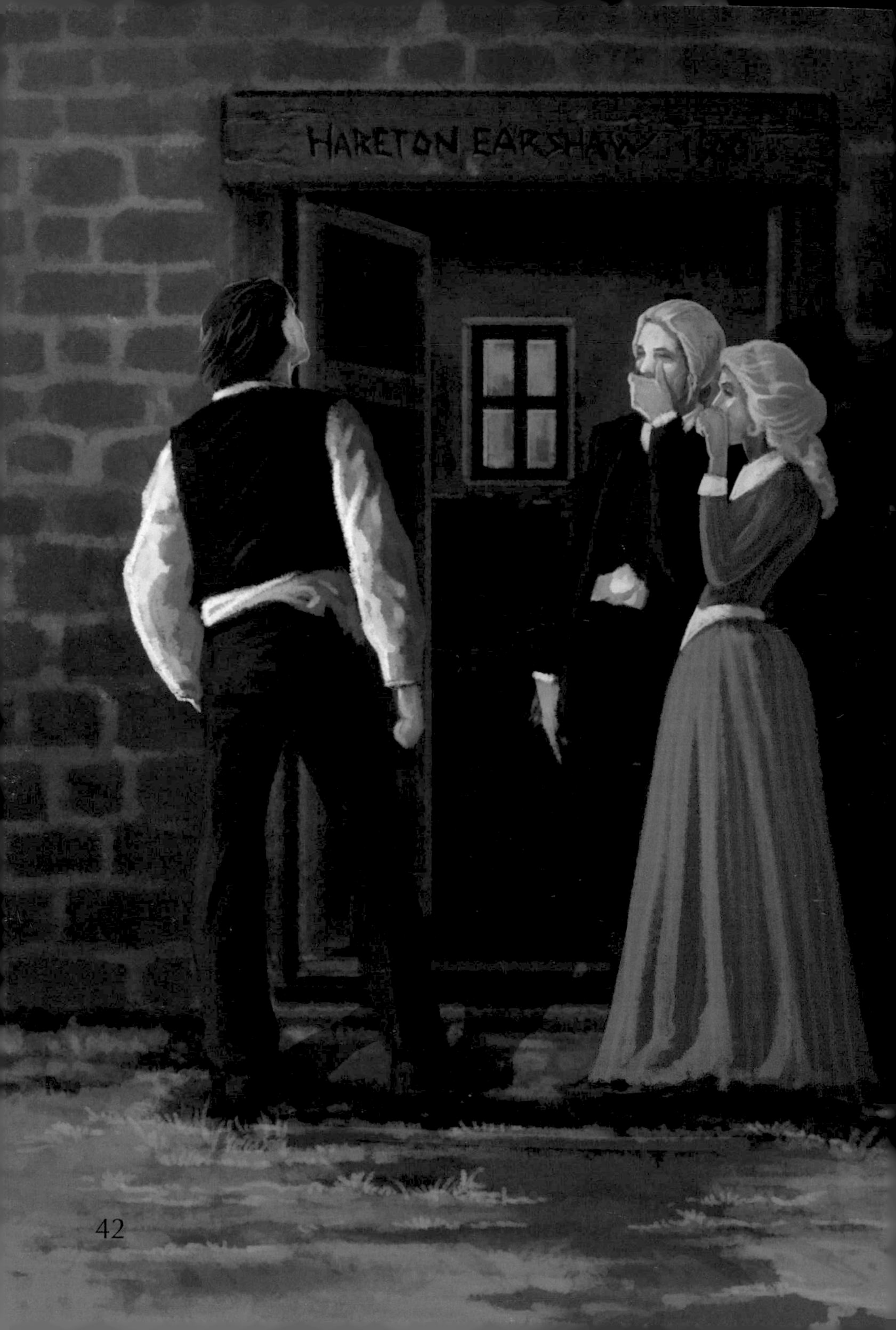
HARETON EARSHAW

So Catherine came to Wuthering Heights to see Linton. She found delight in him – I don't know why. Together they laughed at poor Hareton who, when asked, couldn't read his own name carved above the door. It made me hate the pair even more.

"Are you plotting something wicked, Mr Heathcliff?" asked Nelly.

I couldn't lie. "I want Linton and Catherine to marry," I said. "Then when Edgar dies and Catherine inherits Thrushcross Grange, it will go to her husband, and when he dies it will come to me."

Nelly was horrified. And once Edgar Linton heard where his daughter had spent the afternoon, he forbade her to visit again.

As the winter months came, Linton's health got worse. So too did Edgar's. Word was he'd soon be dead and this news excited me. With Catherine set to inherit, I couldn't wait any longer and went in search of her. I found her walking near the Grange.

"Linton thinks you've abandoned him," I lied. "He dreams of seeing you again."

Hearing this, the vain creature couldn't help but visit. Once I had her under my roof, I bolted the doors. She panicked, wanting to go home to her own father who was seriously ill.

"He'll be miserable without me," Catherine said.

"Good. That's why I'm keeping you here," I remarked. "You'll not leave until you marry Linton."

At which she fell to her knees before me. "Mr Heathcliff, I beg you, have mercy. I love my father dearly. Have you never loved anyone in your life?"

Her question made me shudder. Was she mad to speak like this to me? She knew nothing of my life or who I'd lost, or why the Lintons and the Earnshaws were to blame.

Catherine remained my guest for five days. Servants from the Grange came looking for her but I sent them away. When she finally left, she went as Mrs Heathcliff, Linton's wife. Her father, Edgar, died soon afterwards. Her husband looked sure to follow. And then Thrushcross Grange would be mine. The deed was almost done.

Chapter 7

Once Edgar Linton was buried, I went to Thrushcross Grange. The house wasn't mine yet, but Catherine was my daughter-in-law. And Linton was in need of a nurse.

I found her and Nelly in the library.

"You're to come with me back to Wuthering Heights," I said.

As I'd thought, she'd remained stupidly loyal to Linton. "He's all I've left now," she said. "Though nobody will cry when you die."

Her words meant nothing to me. I was past feeling anything. Yet on the wall was a portrait of her mother, Cathy. It was such a strong likeness that I felt my cold heart warm. In her eyes I saw the spirit that so reminded me of others I'd lost.

When Catherine had gone to pack, I shared a secret with Nelly. "I've left instructions to be buried next to Cathy when I die."

Nelly didn't like my talk. But I begged her to listen. Something was happening, I told her. I'd started to feel Cathy's spirit and others too, as if they were calling for me to join them. I wasn't ill, I told her, though sweat gathered on my forehead. In fact, I'd never felt so alive.

On returning to Wuthering Heights, Catherine discovered how sick Linton was. He tossed and turned and needed her constantly. When finally he died in the middle of the night, I was glad to be rid of him.

For weeks afterwards, Catherine kept to her room. I visited her only once to show her Linton's will, which said he'd left everything to me. This included what, through marriage, he'd inherited from her. Put simply, it meant Thrushcross Grange, at last, was mine.

My revenge was complete. Two respectable cotton-trading families, the Earnshaws and the Lintons, had nothing. Whereas I, an orphan found on the streets of Liverpool, was now the richest landowner in the district. It should've brought me great satisfaction. Yet instead, I felt only tiredness.

About this time, I noticed a change in my house. I'd taken to wandering the moors all day. It was the only place I could find peace. One evening on my return, I saw Catherine teaching Hareton to read. Sensing my presence, they glanced up. And their look was Cathy's look. It made me shiver so much I banished them from my sight.

"Are you ill?" Nelly asked me.

"No," I said. "Yet I sense life is changing."

My tiredness had become overwhelming. How I'd worked all these years to destroy two families, just as mine had once been torn apart! I'd set the Earnshaws and the Lintons against each other. Yet despite this, Catherine and Hareton were fast becoming friends. I had no desire left to fight it.

"Your conscience is catching up with you, sir," Nelly observed.

I believed she was right. In the following days, my tiredness became exhaustion. Yet I couldn't sleep or eat, and still spent my time walking the moors. I saw Cathy and my parents in every blade of grass and every tree. They'd come for me, I knew. And it made me glad to think I'd soon be with them again.

Yet Nelly was concerned, insisting I see a doctor.

How could I?

Peace was fast approaching. Every day Hareton and Catherine grew closer and happier. They dug a garden together, and she, the silly girl, put primroses in his porridge. It was clear their futures lay together.

So I summoned the lawyer to write my will. I had no need for land where I was heading. At last I knew what that name carved above the door truly meant. The Earnshaws had lived here since 1500. As the last surviving family member, Wuthering Heights belonged to Hareton. It wasn't right to take what was his. It didn't make things better.

To Nelly, I repeated my instructions. "Bury me in Gimmerton Churchyard alongside Cathy. Say no kind words over my coffin. And please, don't weep."

"I don't like this talk," she replied.

At dusk, I went to bed – not to my own room, but to Cathy's. I felt so exhausted I was certain I'd sleep forever. I took care to lock the door, as I'd no wish to be disturbed. But Nelly came and called to me, until Hareton – that dear boy – told her to leave me alone.

Before sleep, I had one last task. Taking up pen and paper, I wrote this account of my life. I wanted the world to know I wasn't born evil. Yet it's taken me all my life to learn that love is so much stronger than hate.

Now, at last, I am finished. Putting down my pen, I cross to the window. The sky outside is bright with morning. I open the window to breathe the fresh, sweet air. On the grass below, arms wide in welcome, are Cathy, my mother and my father.

They've come for me. I'm going home.

Wuthering Heights

Mr
Earnshaw

Mrs
Earnshaw

Hindley
Earnshaw

Catherine
Earnshaw

Hareton
Earnshaw

Family Tree

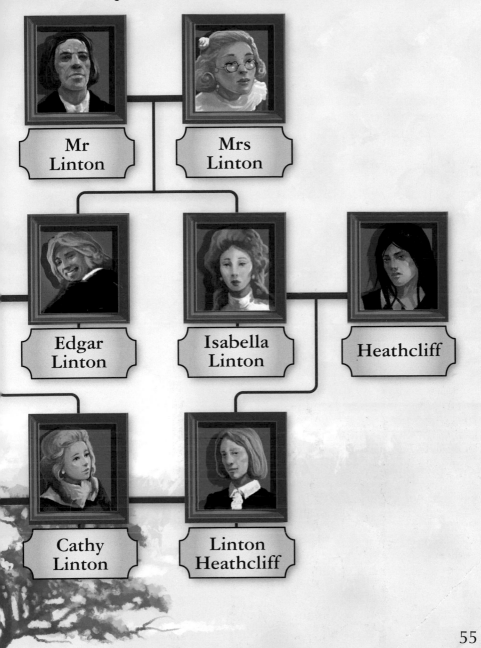

Mr Linton

Mrs Linton

Edgar Linton

Isabella Linton

Heathcliff

Cathy Linton

Linton Heathcliff

Ideas for reading

Written by Clare Dowdall, PhD
Lecturer and Primary Literacy Consultant

Reading objectives:
- identify and discuss themes and conventions in and across a wide range of writing
- draw inferences such as inferring characters' feelings, thoughts and motives from their actions, and justify inferences with evidence
- discuss and evaluate how authors use language, including figurative language, considering the impact on the reader

Spoken language objectives:
- use spoken language to develop understanding through speculating, hypothesising, imagining and exploring ideas

Curriculum links: Geography – place knowledge

Resources: images of the Yorkshire Moors; paints and paper

Build a context for reading
- Show children the front cover. Ask if they've heard of this famous classic story before. Ask them to describe the setting shown in the illustration, and to think about what Wuthering Heights is.
- Challenge them to predict what sort of story this is, based on the title and cover, and explain their ideas.
- Explain that revenge is a key theme in this story. Discuss what revenge means and ask children to give some examples of revenge.

Understand and apply reading strategies
- Read the first paragraph, and discuss what the narrator is saying and what he means by "there's no joy in hate". Explore how it links to the story's theme of revenge.
- Challenge children to a fact-attack. Ask them to read pp2–9 quietly and then work as a group to create a context for their reading by sharing as many key facts about Heathcliff and the theme of revenge as they can.